Glow in the Dark
Stars, Moon, and Clouds

Written by Eugene Bradley Coco
Illustrated by Patti Boyd

A GOLDEN BOOK • NEW YORK

Western Publishing Company, Inc., Racine, Wisconsin 53404

(See back cover for special Glow in the Dark directions!)

One star-filled night as Ethan looked out of his bedroom window, he thought to himself, "I wish those stars could shine just for me."

Then he took a great big sack, a creaky old ladder, and a giant net and sneaked outside.

Ethan set the ladder on a hill, climbed to the top, and swept the stars into the sack. He ran home and put all of the stars into a big tank.

Then he watched them, and he watched them, and he watched them. But the stars didn't shine like they shined in the sky.

"Why don't you shine for me like you shined in the sky?" Ethan asked the stars.

"Because we miss our friend the moon," they replied. "If he were here, then we would be happy and we would shine for you."

So once again Ethan took the great big sack, the creaky old ladder, and the giant net and sneaked outside. He set the ladder on a hill, climbed to the top, and swept the moon into the sack. Ethan ran home and hung the moon next to the stars.

Then he watched them, and he watched them, and he watched them. But the stars still didn't shine like they shined in the sky.

So again Ethan asked the stars, "Why don't you shine for me like you shined in the sky?"

"Because our friend the moon is sad," they replied. "If he was happy, we would be happy. And then we would shine for you."

So Ethan asked the moon, "Why are you sad?"
And the moon said, "Because I miss my friends the clouds. If they were here, then I wouldn't be sad."

So one more time Ethan took the great big sack, the creaky old
ladder, and the giant net and sneaked outside. He set the ladder
on a hill, climbed to the top, and swept the clouds into the sack.
Ethan ran home and pinned the clouds next to the moon
and stars.

Then he watched them, and he watched them, and he watched them. But even with the clouds there, the stars still didn't shine the way they shined in the sky.

"I did as you asked," Ethan said to the stars. "But you still don't shine for me like you shined in the sky."

"That's because the clouds are unhappy," replied the stars. "If they are unhappy, then the moon is unhappy. And if the moon is unhappy, then we are unhappy. And if we are unhappy, then we cannot shine for you."

So Ethan asked the clouds, "Why are you unhappy?"
"We miss the sky," they said. "If the sky were here, then we would be happy."

Ethan thought for a moment.

"The sky is too big for me to carry," he said at last. "I cannot bring it to you."

"But you can bring all of us to the sky," said the stars. "If you put us back in the sky, we will all be happy. And then we will shine for you."

"And why is that?" asked Ethan.

"Because the sky is our home," said the stars. "And that's where we belong."

So for the last time, Ethan took the great big sack filled with the stars, the moon, and the clouds, the creaky old ladder, and the giant net, and went outside.

Ethan set the ladder on a hill and opened up the sack. With both hands, Ethan threw the moon back into the sky. Then he took a deep breath and blew the clouds next to the moon. Finally Ethan sprinkled the stars across the sky and climbed back down the ladder.

Before his eyes, Ethan could see the moon smiling, the clouds dancing, and the stars shining, brighter than ever.

"The stars were right," said Ethan as he began to dance beneath the glowing sky. "They belong in the sky. That is their home. Now they are happy."

And Ethan was happy, too.